Magical Moon Cat

Jax opened her mouth, then quickly closed it, surprised to discover that she had changed her mind about Ruby-Rose. She wasn't any fonder of Ruby-Rose, but she liked Betty Boo, her dog. *Betty Boo can't be happy until Ruby-Rose is happy, Jax* realized. *If that poor little dog gets any more stressed, she'll go totally bald! They both need our help.*

Magical Moon Cat

Moonbeans
and the Shining Star

Annie Dalton

USBORNE

With thanks to all the kind humans who took my dog for walks while
I was writing this book; you know who you are!

First published in 2012 by Usborne Publishing Ltd., Usborne House, 83-85 Saffron Hill, London EC1N 8RT, England. www.usborne.com

Text copyright © Annie Dalton, 2012 Cover illustration by Tuesday Mourning. Inside illustrations by Katie Lovell. Illustration copyright © Usborne Publishing Ltd, 2012

The right of Annie Dalton to be identified as the author of this work has been asserted by her in accordance with the Copyright, Designs and Patents Act, 1988.

The name Usborne and the devices are Trade Marks of Usborne Publishing Ltd.

A CIP catalogue record for this book is available from the British Library.

ISBN 9781409526322

JFMAM JASOND/12 00498/1

Printed in Dongguan, Guangdong, China.

Contents

Secrets and stardust

1

Summer had arrived early in Goose Green. Cars drove by with their windows down, letting out blasts of music and thumping beats. Jax and Lilia got so hot walking home from school that they had to peel off their hideous bottle-green cardigans and tie them around their waists.

Once, long ago, Goose Green had been a peaceful little village with a village green and a pond. Now it smelled of traffic fumes and a zillion different kinds of takeaway. The first time Jax saw where her mum had brought her to live, she burst out crying. She thought it was a total dump. She missed her dad (she would always miss her dad) and her mum was working too hard doing up her new café to pay her much attention.

That first night she had huddled under her quilt, trying to shut out the wails of emergency vehicles racing through the dark. *Nothing magic could ever happen here,* she thought.

But Jax was wrong. Magic had happened. In fact it was still happening to her, right here in the noisy heart of the city, and it was making her life *really* complicated.

It had all started so suddenly. One minute  Jax had been spying on her neighbours through her dad's telescope, the next minute, the water in her goldfish tank had turned a blazing pink as a lightning ball hurtled past her window. It wasn't normal lightning, though; Jax had realized that at once. It was a spaceship.

Some people might have panicked. Not Jax. She'd been waiting for this moment ever since her scientist dad explained that an alien was simply someone she hadn't met yet. But she never imagined that her alien would turn out to be a mind-reading moon kitten! His name was Moonbeans and he had been living with Jax for almost six weeks.

This was the secret that Jax had been hugging to herself every day while she was at school. This was why she was always the first person out of the school gate at home time; she was hurrying home to her magical little moon cat.

Lost in her own thoughts, she didn't notice her friend giving her huffy looks. Suddenly Lilia burst out, "Why do you have to walk so fast? You're always in a mad hurry to get home."

Jax felt her stomach drop. "I…I just want to get home and take off these hot prickly clothes," she stuttered.

"Not every single day, you don't," Lilia objected. "Even when it's not hot, you're like, *rush-rush-rush*."

Jax swallowed. "I already explained about that. I have to go home to feed Beans. I told you, my mum said I could keep him just so long as I look after him."

"We've got cats too, you know," Lilia snapped, quick as a flash. "Just because you've got a cat, it doesn't mean you can't come round to mine after school."

"I do come round to yours."

"You came *once*! You said my house was like cupcake heaven. That was the one and only time!" Lilia was fighting back tears.

They had almost reached the pelican crossing. Jax felt bad about upsetting her friend, but she was even more desperate to get back to Beans. A group of giggling girls went rushing over the crossing and she secretly wished she could be rushing with them; if she ran all the way without stopping, she'd be back home in five minutes max. But Jax couldn't leave her friend while she was still so upset.

"When you stopped Conrad bullying me that time, I thought you wanted to be my friend," Lilia was saying tearfully. "But you can't really like me, or you wouldn't make excuses about feeding kittens."

Jax was feeling like a
really bad person now.
She longed to explain
that her kitten Beans
was nothing like Lilia's

kitties, Poppy and Petal. But she couldn't,
because it wasn't actually her secret to tell.

Wanting to make things up to her, Jax gave
Lilia a beaming smile. "Of course I like you,
you wally! And I honestly haven't been avoiding
you. It's just that sometimes my mum needs me
to help in the café."

The first two sentences were almost
completely true. Jax hadn't deliberately been
avoiding Lilia; she had genuinely enjoyed going
to tea at Lilia's house. It was just that she spent
all day with Lilia, and after school she was
desperate to run straight home to Beans.

Then she sneaked another look at poor Lilia

and decided she was just being selfish. "I promise I'll come round to yours tomorrow," she told Lilia. "Or…I know! Tomorrow, why don't you come back with me? Your mum helps out at the café on Fridays, doesn't she?" *That way I'll still get to see Beans*, she thought.

Jax could have invited Lilia to come back with her before, but she got so stressed having to pretend that Beans was just an ordinary cat. It wasn't easy living with a secret moon kitten. She just had to make one silly little slip and the whole world would know.

I can do this, Jax told herself. *I've just got to be really careful, then everything will be okay.*

Lilia didn't seem to notice that Jax had switched plans at the last minute. "Okay! It's a deal!" She beamed back at Jax, her bad mood instantly forgotten. Linking arms, they walked on towards the crossing, where they usually went their separate ways.

Lilia gave her hand an apologetic squeeze. "Sorry if I was a drama queen. I got to thinking I just wasn't cool enough to be your friend."

"You are bonkers, Lilia, you know that?" Jax told her. "I'm so not cool!"

Lilia blinked at her. "You are, though. You live over that cool café with your mum. You're, like, the coolest girl in our school."

Jax laughed. "People didn't think my mum and me were so cool when we took it over, remember? Anyway, the main reason our café is super-cool is because your mum is a cake-baking genius and makes us all those brilliant cupcakes."

"Actually, that's true!" Lilia agreed, cheering up. "I should have listened to my mum. She kept telling me I was being silly. She *said* you were probably rushing home to help your mum. She said it must be hard for you losing your dad. I miss *my* dad loads and I still see him every weekend!"

Jax felt her smile freeze. The idea of Lilia and her mum talking together about her dad made her feel as if she suddenly couldn't breathe.

Lilia didn't seem to notice that Jax had gone quiet. "Mum said your dad was some kind of space scientist," she chattered.

Jax gave a subdued little nod. "My dad knew everything about outer space." She longed to make Lilia understand how special and wonderful her dad was, but she couldn't find the right words.

Lilia scrunched up her face and started

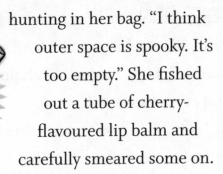

hunting in her bag. "I think outer space is spooky. It's too empty." She fished out a tube of cherry-flavoured lip balm and carefully smeared some on.

"I *love* it," Jax said fiercely. "And for your information, space isn't empty. There are stars and meteorites and black holes and space junk. There's loads of cool things up in space."

Lilia gave a surprised giggle. "Wow, I never knew you were a space geek, Jax. You'll be talking about slimy green aliens next!" She pulled a funny face. "Gross."

But Jax didn't think this was funny. Without meaning to, she clenched her fists. "Why does everyone think aliens are slimy and green?" she said angrily. "My dad said there was no reason aliens had to be scary.

He said they could even be, you know, really *cute!*"

Dad had never said aliens might be cute. Jax had let herself get carried away, but she didn't care. It made her livid the way people talked about aliens. Beans was an alien and he wasn't green or slimy. He was the best thing that had ever happened to Jax in her whole life.

For a long moment Lilia stared at Jax, open-mouthed. Then she shrieked with laughter. "Cute aliens! Jax, that is SO funny!"

"Why is it funny?" Jax demanded. "We're all made out of the same stardust anyway, my dad said!"

Lilia's eyes went wide. "I never knew people were made from stardust."

"Everything in this whole universe is made out of it – including aliens," she added recklessly. *Stop it, Jax,* she told herself. But she couldn't stop. She was furious.

Now Lilia looked shocked. "Are you saying we're the same as aliens?"

"Alien is only a word, Lilia! It just means 'stranger'! Somebody you don't know yet!" Jax was almost shouting.

Lilia seemed bewildered. "But, Jax, why would anyone ever want to know an *alien?*"

The little green man on the crossing had started to beep. Jax seized her chance to get away. "Sorry, I've got to go! See you tomorrow, Lilia," she gabbled.

She tore across the crossing and didn't stop until she reached the launderette. Mum was always telling Jax she had to control her temper, and had Jax listened? She had not. She had let herself get so steaming mad that she had almost told Lilia the truth about Beans.

The pavement smelled of hot soapsuds and scorched cotton from the launderette. It was a homely kind of smell, and as she breathed it in, Jax felt herself gradually calming down.

She had stopped herself from blurting out her secret – just. She hadn't betrayed herself or Beans. He was safe at home, waiting for her to come back from school so they could catch up with each other's news.

This thrilling thought pulled her breathlessly along the street, until she finally saw the café's stylish new windows sparkling in the sun.

When her mum took over Dolly's Diner, there had been grease on the walls and mice running around in the storeroom. Now the mice had gone, the café had been scrubbed from top to bottom, and been given a fresh coat of sunflower-yellow paint, and a brand new name: the Dream Café.

Through the open door, Jax could hear mechanical chomping sounds. Mum was standing behind the counter, feeding slippery mango slices and prickly chunks of pineapple into a giant juicer.

Getting Mum's café up and running had been hard work, but now her business was booming. Customers came from all over to sip frothy cappuccinos and try Lilia's mum's fabulous cupcakes.

Jax went to join her mum behind the counter. "Hi!"

Mum looked surprised. "You're home early, Ellie Mae!"

"I'm Jax now, remember?" Jax told her for the ten-billionth time.

"I can't call you Jax," said her mum, also for the ten-billionth time. "Ellie Mae is such a beautiful name."

Jax rolled her eyes. "Name me *one* world-famous scientist or explorer called Ellie Mae!"

"With a name like Ellie Mae Jackson our daughter can be anything she wants," Mum said softly. "That's what your dad used to say."

If Jax shut her eyes she could still hear the smile in Dad's voice as he said those words. For a few moments she leaned against her mum, then Mum gave herself a brisk shake and went back to feeding fruit into the juicer. "So how was school today?"

Jax sneaked a piece of pineapple. "School was school," she said. "I'm going to find Beans."

The backyard was tiny, so he was easy to

21

spot. Her little cat wasn't lolling in the sun. He was sitting up poker-straight with his back to her, his ears twitching at every sound. Balancing trustingly on his head was a tiny baby bird.

Jax had to stuff her knuckles into her mouth to stop herself laughing with pure delight. Her dad was right. Aliens are real, and they can also be cute. And Jax was looking at one very cute alien right now.

The Purr of Power

2

Soon after Jax and her mother took over
the café, a blackbird had made her nest
in their twisty old lilac tree. After the eggs
had hatched out, they had watched her flying
in and out with food for her fledglings. Jax
guessed this baby bird must be learning how
to fly, but it was still too young and weak to
get back to its nest.

As she watched from the doorway, Jax could
hear a bumblebee buzzing in and out of some
honeysuckle flowers. The sound was gradually
swallowed by the steady throb of Moonbeans

purring. Like ordinary cats, moon cats purred when they were happy. They also purred when they were doing magic – just like Beans was doing now. Jax jokingly called it "the Purr of Power". When he first arrived on Earth, Moonbeans's powers had been a bit iffy, but he'd been practising with Jax every day and he was getting loads better.

It's working, she thought. She could see the yard gradually filling with a soft pink shimmer. The baby bird seemed to feel the magic too. He put his head on one side and gave a sharp *cheep*.

The air will hold you up, Beans told the bird. *Spread your wings and you'll remember how to fly.* From the day they met, Jax had always heard Moonbeans's thoughts, just as if he'd spoken them out loud.

The little bird gave a hopeful flap, lost its balance, and almost fell off Moonbeans's head.

Jax felt all her
muscles tense.
Someone else
was watching
the little fledgling.

A tortoiseshell cat was slinking along the wall,
her green eyes glittering like glass. With her
eyes fixed unblinkingly on the bird, the cat
crept stealthily closer.

Jax wanted to clap her hands and yell to
scare it off, but if she did that she'd interrupt
the magic. *I can't watch,* she thought, and her
mouth went dry with fear for the baby bird.
It was too young, its wings were too weak – it
didn't stand a chance.

Do you mind? I'm concentrating, Beans told
her, and he went on steadily, patiently purring,
until Jax could feel the moon magic tingling
through her veins.

After some more desperate wobbling, the
baby blackbird felt brave enough to try again.
Jax watched, amazed, as it lifted itself up onto
its toes, flapped its weedy little wings twice,
spread them wide, then flew as straight as an

 arrow up to its nest in the
lilac tree.

"*Tweet!*" it shouted
down proudly. "*Tweet,
tweet, tweet!*"

The tortoiseshell cat stalked away, her tail
waving disdainfully.

Beans trotted up to Jax as if nothing unusual
had happened. He weaved around her ankles,
purring; not one of his magic purrs, just an
ordinary pleased-to-see-you purr.

She crouched down so he could bump noses
with her.

"Beans, that was SO cool how you saved that

bird!" Jax was so proud of him she could have cried. "I wish we had a camcorder. I could have put it on YouTube." Then she quickly shook her head. "Bad idea! We don't want some creepy alien hunter to come looking for you!"

"I'm melting in these things. I'm going in," she said abruptly. "Coming?"

Upstairs, all the rooms were hot and stuffy. Jax pushed up her bedroom window to let in some air. She quickly changed into old cotton cut-offs and a faded red T-shirt, and sighed with relief.

For a few minutes Jax just enjoyed feeling cool, with the summer breeze blowing in through the window. *I'm always happy when I'm with Moonbeans*, she thought.

At that moment, he was making himself at home on her quilt, kneading it with his claws in the way that drove Mum mad. He was

27

purring the extra-loud
tea-kettle purr that
he saved for
moments when he
was completely happy.

Jax lay down beside him, breathing in the faint jelly-bean smell that the little moon cat had brought with him from his world. This delicious other-worldly scent was part of the reason she'd named him Moonbeans. Beans didn't have a name until he met Jax. He'd explained that moon cats don't see the point of names. Jax thought maybe it had something to do with them being able to read minds.

She began stroking him gently the wrong way so she could admire the shimmery tiger stripes hidden underneath his fur. "Do all moon cats have secret tiger stripes, or just you?" she asked.

Mine are hidden because I'm only half moon-cat, said Beans. *My mum wears her tiger stripes on the outside.*

"What about the sparkles in your fur?"

All moon cats have them, Beans told her. *You should see us when we're all together in the moonlight. My world has five moons, so our moonlight is extra bright.*

"Your world has five moons! You never told me that!" Jax was enchanted. These were the moments she dreamed about when she was at school – just her and Beans chatting in their own little world. Jax did really like Lilia…but it wouldn't be the same if she was here.

Jax knew that Moonbeans hadn't come to Earth just to be her little pet alien, though. He had been sent on a mission by mysterious beings he called "the Aunts", who wanted to make Planet Earth a happier place to live for humans and other life forms. The first phase of Beans's mission, getting the Dream Café up and running, had been a roaring success.

Jax was suddenly desperate to know what was going to happen next. "Beans, now Mum's café is doing so well, isn't it time we got our next mission?"

The Aunts will tell us when it's time, he told her.

"How will they know, though?" she objected. "They're millions of light years away on another world."

I don't know how they know, admitted Beans. *I suppose it's because they are so wise.*

"Are they *real* aunts, though?"

Of course they're real. Did you think I'd made them up? Beans seemed offended.

"Don't get in a huff! I meant are they actual

relatives, or is it like a big cosmic organization kind of thing?"

They're not relatives like you humans have, and they're not an organization. They're the Aunts of every moon cat that has ever lived or will ever live on my world, Beans explained.

Conversations about the Aunts tended to make Jax feel dizzy. "So they're really old then?" she said.

Older than the stars, Beans said.

I expect that's how they got so wise, Jax thought. She wondered if the Aunts looked like big cats or if they were more like small tigers? There was so much about Moonbeans's world that she didn't know.

"I'd love to visit your world," she told him wistfully.

I'd love to show it to you, said Moonbeans.

"You could beam me pictures," she suggested. Jax didn't just hear Beans's thoughts in words. Sometimes she saw pictures too. But they had learned that this worked better if they were both deliberately trying.

Maybe. Beans biffed her with his hard little skull, changing the subject. *Now, tell me three interesting things to tell the Aunts.*

This was a game Beans had invented. Jax had been complaining about leaving him to go to school. Beans told her to look out for interesting Goose Green info to send back to the Aunts.

"It's too hot to play that now," Jax moaned. "Anyway, the only interesting thing here is you. Goose Green is boring!"

Moonbeans didn't agree. His mum had been visiting Goose Green with a secret delegation

of moon cats when she fell in love with the
handsome Earth cat who became his dad.
Perhaps that was why everything about this
world was so fascinating to Beans, Jax thought.
He got excited by things she scarcely bothered
to notice: the sunrise over city rooftops; the
way birds sang after the rain (moon birds didn't
sing apparently).
He even got excited
about talking to
Jax's goldfish,
Brad!

Jax could feel Moonbeans fixing her with
his unblinking amber stare. He was still
waiting for her to come up with her three
things. She knew he'd keep staring until she
gave in.

"Okay," she sighed. She thought for a
minute. "Got one. On the way to school this

morning, we saw a super-sized squirrel raiding a bucket of fried chicken someone had just dumped in the gutter. Mum said you could tell it ate a LOAD of junk food. It was a monster!"

Jax wasn't sure why the Aunts would want to hear about a junk-food eating squirrel, but Beans seemed pleased.

Two more, he prompted.

Jax twiddled a strand of her hair while she thought, then she started to grin. "Actually something really funny happened at school. You remember Conrad? Mrs. Chaudhary sent him outside."

He wasn't bullying Lilia again? asked Beans.

Jax shook her head, remembering how she and Beans had put a stop to Conrad's bullying ways. Later, no one was sure if they really had seen the new girl turn into a flashing, sparkling, karate-kicking girl firework; but everyone agreed that Conrad was a changed boy.

"He wasn't being a bully, he was just being Conrad – you know how he gets," Jax told Beans. "Mrs. Chaudhary says he has too much energy for his own good. She told him to run twice round the playground then come back in. Conrad is so cheeky!" she said, giggling. "He ran twice around the playground, only he did it backwards! When Mrs. Chaudhary told him off, he said, 'Miss, you just said run! You never said which way!'"

Beans looked tickled. *I like Conrad.*

"He gets on with almost everybody in my class now," Jax said, then quickly corrected herself. "Everybody except Ruby-Rose. She's the

one causing all the
trouble nowadays."

*Is Ruby-Rose the
girl who has a little
fluffy dog?*

Moonbeans was being tactful, Jax thought
gratefully. He could have said: "Oh, Ruby-Rose
– that's the girl you secretly spied on when you
first arrived in Goose Green!" Jax had told
Beans absolutely everything that had happened
to her the day he came hurtling out of the sky
and into her life, though the part about using
her dad's telescope to spy on her neighbours
had made her hot with embarrassment. Dad
wouldn't have approved of her using his
telescope to spy on her fellow humans.

I'm a different person now, she told herself.
That was before Moonbeans came.

Aloud, she said, "Ruby-Rose just loves to

get people into trouble. No one in my class likes her. You just have to breathe on her and she has a hissy fit."

Did she have a hissy fit today?

"She has one *every* day," said Jax with feeling. "The smallest thing sets her off."

What set her off today?

"Actually it was Conrad! Every time Conrad does a drawing, he has to sing. He doesn't, you know, really belt it out, he just sings under his breath. Lilia thinks he doesn't even know he's doing it. Anyway, he started singing and Ruby-Rose went bonkers! She burst into tears and went running to Mrs. Chaudhary and said he was deliberately singing the Sparkle Fluff song to make her look stupid! Miss believed her – teachers always believe Ruby-Rose.
That's why she sent Conrad outside."

Beans seemed baffled. *The Sparkle Fluff song?*

Putting on a cute little-girl voice, Jax sang, "'Sparkle Fluff is full of stuff that little fairies love.' It's an advert for a pudding in a tub," she explained. "It's fluffy, like marshmallow, and it's got sparkles in – that's why it's called Sparkle Fluff.

Mum won't buy it because it's got chemicals."

Why did Ruby-Rose think Conrad was trying to make her look stupid? Beans pondered.

Jax shrugged. "Lilia said that Ruby-Rose did the voice for the little cartoon fairy in the commercial. She does all these drama classes after school." She gave Beans a mischievous grin. "That's probably why she's so good at fooling teachers."

Jax didn't want to think about Ruby-Rose for a minute more than she had to. She jumped off the bed with a bounce. "Is that my three interesting things?"

Yes, thank you, said Beans politely.

"Good, because I'm starving! I'm going to beg Mum for a triple-chocolate cupcake. Coming?"

Beans followed her as far as the downstairs hall then he suddenly stopped. *There's someone I need to see,* he said.

Jax was disappointed. She had just assumed they'd spend the rest of the day together. *Get used to it, Jax,* she told herself. *He's a moon cat on a mission. Not a cuddly little pet.*

She wondered if he was going to see Rumble, the battle-scarred old tomcat Beans hung around with sometimes. Not even the Aunts knew this, but Beans had another personal reason for wanting to visit Earth: he had always longed to meet his dad. And the old street cat had promised to use his contacts to help track him down.

"Will you be back before I go to bed?" Jax asked him hopefully.

Beans had stopped listening. He was gingerly approaching the cat flap. He could have used magic to get out of the house, but Jax and Beans wanted their neighbours to believe that he was a normal kitten. Unfortunately Beans *really* hated his cat flap and treated it like a cunning beast with snapping jaws that had to be outwitted. As he preferred to fight his cat-flap battles in private, Jax tactfully left him to it.

As she tiptoed away, she heard him hurl

himself violently at the door. There was a lot of desperate scrabbling, followed by a shattering *THWACK!* as he finally disappeared.

Poor Beans, she thought, giggling. She was still smirking as she slipped through the side door into the café. Then she suddenly stopped in her tracks. Was it her imagination, or was their café looking unusually *shimmery*?

When her mum started renovating Dolly's Diner, some local people had complained. They thought Mum was going to turn it into some snobby upscale café. They wanted to keep Dolly's the way it was, chip fat and all. Then Moonbeans came, and suddenly everyone started offering to help. Conrad's big brother Lenny came to finish the decorating. Mei Lee from the Red Hot Wok donated her spare freezer. Lilia's mum Nadia turned out to be a total genius at making cupcakes and cookies.

If Jax hadn't known better, she might have thought all those things just happened by chance…

After the café opened, Mum's customers constantly commented on its friendly vibe. They saw Moonbeans strolling and purring between the tables but they didn't make a connection. They thought they just kept coming back because Jax's mum served good coffee and cakes.

Only Jax and Beans knew the truth. The Aunts had a daring and ambitious project for Planet Earth and they had chosen Moonbeans and Jax to put it into action right here in Goose Green. Jax still had no clue which local human the Aunts would ask them to help next, but she knew it would be

someone who came into Mum's café.
Moonbeans had explained that the Dream
Café was a crucial part of the
Aunts' plan.

The thought made
her heart beat faster.
Anyone could walk
into a café. A princess
could walk into a café.
Someone could burst in
begging them to hide her from kidnappers.
Whoever it was, it would be someone in real
trouble, the kind of trouble that only a nine-
year-old girl with a magical moon cat could fix.

Is it you? Jax asked each of the customers
silently.

She wasn't imagining the glimmer, the
café seemed to be getting more shimmery
by the minute…and were those *pink sparkles*

43

falling softly through the air?

It's happening! The mission is starting. Jax hugged herself with excitement. She noticed her mum hurrying over to greet two new customers who had just walked in. And the pink sparkles faded like a dream as she recognized the scowling face of Ruby-Rose.

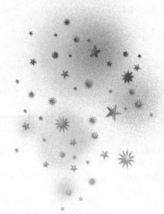

Mummy's little star

3

*C*arefully not looking at Ruby-Rose, Jax made her way between the tables until she reached the counter.

Still keeping her back turned, she stared intently into the display cabinet, pretending she was deciding which of Lilia's mum's fabulous cupcakes she fancied most. She already knew which cake she wanted: a triple-chocolate cupcake. She just wanted to make it totally clear that she was ignoring Ruby-Rose. At school Ruby-Rose always acted like she was the boss of everyone, even Mrs. Chaudhary.

Well, she wasn't the boss of Ellie Mae Jackson,
Jax thought fiercely. Everything about
Ruby-Rose rubbed Jax up the wrong way, for
instance, the way she had just come waltzing
into their café wearing her shiny dance leotard,
like some off-duty celeb. Then there were

Ruby-Rose's bunches
which looked like
spaniel's ears tied
up with ribbons.
She disliked
Ruby-Rose, but she
disliked Ruby-Rose's mother even more,
because of how she treated their dog. Jax had
seen Ruby-Rose's mum walking it around the
square. *She never even looked at the poor dog,* Jax
thought angrily, *just dragged it along on its lead
like a doggy suitcase-on-wheels.* Jax loved all
animals and she couldn't understand why

anyone would go to all the trouble of getting a dog and then totally ignore it.

I'm so glad my mum looks like a real mum, Jax thought. Ruby-Rose's mum looked like a mum someone had bought from a catalogue. *I bet it takes her hours to put her make-up on,* she smirked spitefully.

While she was pretending to choose her cake, Jax heard her mum go over to Ruby-Rose and her mum. They must have picked a table by the window. Ruby-Rose's mum immediately started complaining that there were too many different kinds of coffee to choose from. Eventually she decided on a skinny latte. "I'm really careful with my calories," she told Jax's mum. "So is my little girl."

"Is this the first time you've come into the café?" Jax could tell Mum was trying to be friendly. "I don't think I've seen you before."

"Ruby-Rose has been pestering me to come for weeks, haven't you, sweetie? This afternoon we had some time to kill before her next dance class, so I thought we might as well give you a try."

Give us a try? How rude! Jax thought, and she swung round to give them both a glare.

"Ruby-Rose goes to Suzie Dazzle's School for the Performing Arts just across the road," Ruby-Rose's mum explained.

Jax walked past Suzie Dazzle's every day. It was in an old converted church. In the afternoons you heard the thunder of tiny tap-shoes against bare wooden boards and a female voice shouting: "Darlings, *darlings!*

Tap, shuffle, *hop*, NOT shuffle, hop, *tap*!!"

"Ruby does all her performing arts classes with Suzie: drama, tap, ballet. She spends more time with Suzie than she does in her own home, don't you, sweetie?" Ruby-Rose's mum patted her daughter's hand.

"So long as she enjoys it," Mum said politely.

"Ruby-Rose *loves* the performing arts," said Ruby-Rose's mum sharply. "She's Mummy's little star, aren't you?"

Ruby-Rose gave a tight nod. So far she hadn't said a word, possibly because her mum didn't let her get a word in.

"Has your little girl got a special talent?" Ruby-Rose's mum asked Jax's mum abruptly.

"She does karate," Ruby-Rose said, to Jax's surprise.

Ruby-Rose's mum did a mock shudder. "We'd better not get on the wrong side of that

49

little girl then, had we, Ruby-Rose?"

Jax held her breath, waiting for Ruby-Rose to say something about Jax turning into a karate-kicking girl firework, but she just muttered, "I wish she'd teach me some."

"Don't be silly, Ruby-Rose," said her mum sharply. "When would you need to use karate?"

Mum was still patiently waiting to take their order. "What would you like to drink?" she asked Ruby-Rose.

Before Ruby-Rose could speak, her mum said quickly, "She'll have sparkling water."

"Would either of you like anything to eat?" asked Mum.

Ruby-Rose sneaked a longing look at the display cabinet.

Her mum clicked her tongue. "Calories, sweetie, remember!" She gave her daughter's hand another pat. Jax saw Ruby-Rose give her dance bag a savage kick under the table where her mum wouldn't see.

Jax waited for Mum to finish serving them, and then she asked for her cupcake. Leaning on the counter, she ate it very slowly, enjoying every chocolatey crumb, while Ruby-Rose pretended not to notice.

As she and Ruby-Rose went on pretending to ignore each other, Jax started to get the giggles. She almost put out her chocolatey tongue at Ruby-Rose to see what she'd do. But just at that moment Ruby-Rose said in her loud clear stage-school voice, "I'm SO glad you didn't buy me one of those cakes, Mummy. I wouldn't want to get all *fat and ugly*!" And Ruby-Rose looked straight at Jax and mimed someone blowing up like a big fat balloon.

Ruby-Rose's mum didn't notice her daughter's bad behaviour. She was looking at her watch. "Is that the time?" she exclaimed in a loud voice. "I've got to drop you off at Suzie's, then I'm taking Betty Boo to the vet's. My daughter's dog is costing us a fortune," she told everyone in the café. "She's *always* ill."

And I thought my mum was embarrassing, thought Jax. She would have felt genuinely sorry for Ruby-Rose, if she hadn't just called Jax fat and ugly.

Ruby-Rose gloomily slung her dance bag over her shoulder. On the side of her bag in glittering letters it said: Shining Star. As Ruby-Rose followed her mum out of the café, Jax didn't think she looked much like a shining star. She just looked like a tired little kid in a leotard.

At bedtime, Moonbeans still hadn't returned.

He's probably still hanging out with Rumble,
Jax thought. To her secret disgust, the stinky
old street cat had become a good friend of
Beans. Almost everyone
was a good friend of
Beans: urban foxes,
passing dogs, baby birds.
Jax got the impression
that Beans loved everyone

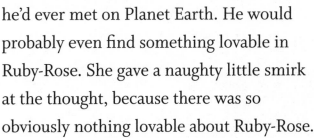

he'd ever met on Planet Earth. He would
probably even find something lovable in
Ruby-Rose. She gave a naughty little smirk
at the thought, because there was so
obviously nothing lovable about Ruby-Rose.

Jax put on her summer PJs, and left her
window open a small crack, just wide enough
for a little moon cat to slip through. She never
totally relaxed until she knew Beans was safely

home. Moonbeans might be magic but he was from another world and Jax wasn't sure he understood about traffic. Plus Jax had a secret and terrible worry that someone – an alien hunter or an evil scientist – might kidnap him, and then she would never see her little moon cat again.

She dozed uneasily, hearing every sound that floated up from the city streets below. A warm breeze blew through the window, bringing traffic fumes, spicy takeaway smells and the faintest whiff of honeysuckle. Jax drowsily pictured Beans prowling down fire escapes, over rooftops and through back gardens, and mentally begged the Aunts to keep him safe.

At last she heard a soft thud as Beans landed on her floor. He jumped onto her bed and threw himself down beside her, purring. Jax stretched and yawned, pretending she had been fast asleep. "How was Rumble? Has he put the word out about your dad?"

I wasn't with Rumble, he said, to her surprise.

Then where had he been? Jax wondered. Beans was being annoyingly mysterious, even for him.

His next words made her heart leap.

But I have got some news from the Aunts, he announced.

I knew it! she thought. That must be why the café had gone all super-sparkly. Jax and her moon cat were so in tune that she had actually seen and felt the Aunts' new instructions being transmitted to Goose Green!

She sat up, wide awake now. "Who do they want us to help?"

The Aunts just tell us when it's time, Moonbeans said confusingly. *They don't choose who we help.*

Jax thought he could have explained this before. "Then how will we know who they are?" she asked, bewildered.

We have to wait to be asked. Moonbeans delicately licked a front paw.

She burst out laughing. "Not to be horrible, Beans, but who would ask a little alien cat for help?"

Beans fixed her with a cool stare. *You're assuming humans are the only life forms who ever need help.*

Jax couldn't believe her ears. "You don't mean someone's asked you already!" *Someone or* **something**, she thought, with a gulp. This was just so typical of Beans. While she was dreaming of princesses, Beans was getting friendly with a "life form". And if she knew Beans, it would be something smelly and rank.

Jax noticed that Beans was carefully avoiding looking at her, which meant she'd guessed right. "Exactly what kind of 'life form' are we talking about?" she asked gloomily. "Animal, vegetable, mineral?" Jax wasn't sure how you'd actually help a mineral.

Animal, said Beans. *A sad, troubled little dog.*

"You want us to help a dog?"

A dog wants us to help her human, Moonbeans corrected patiently. *Betty Boo says she's tried to make her human happy, but she can't do it by herself.*

Jax gave a grumpy laugh. "You'd be sad and troubled too if your name was Betty Boo—"

She suddenly realized what she'd said. "You are joking!" she said in horror. But she knew he wasn't. Out of all the zillions of life forms in Goose Green, they had to help Ruby-Rose.

In her dreams, Jax was shouting at the Aunts out of her bedroom window: "Do you even *know* Ruby-Rose? Well I do, and she is not even a tiny bit nice! There must be loads of nicer people we could be helping."

The Aunts smiled back at her from their tiny moonlit world.

Betty Boo needs you, they said firmly, *and so does Ruby-Rose.*

Jax woke to find she had thrown all her pillows angrily on the floor. Beans had helped himself to one, and now he was balancing on it like a surfer, trying to wash the tricky bit under his chin.

Bad dream? he asked.

Jax didn't bother to answer. She stormed over to her chest of drawers. "We can't start the mission till Monday anyway!" she snapped. "Grandpa's coming to stay this weekend, remember."

Beans knew and Jax knew that Grandpa was not coming to stay. Each time he promised to visit them, Mum would make plans for fun things they could all do together, but then he'd ring up the night before with another excuse. Before Mum and Jax had moved to Goose Green, they lived just a few streets away from Grandpa and Jax had seen him almost every day. He had been totally against Mum taking Jax away to start a new life on the other side of the city. But then he'd seemed to come around

– he'd actually showed up for the Dream Café's big launch. That was the last time he'd come to see them, though. Jax was sure he really missed seeing her and her mum, because they really, *really* missed him. It was a total mystery.

Beans lightly patted her cheek with his paw to get her attention.

We could start the mission tonight.

"No, actually, Beans, we couldn't, because I promised Lilia she could come back after school," she said, slamming drawers. Jax was trying to punish Beans for agreeing to help Ruby-Rose behind her back, but he just said, *Good, I like Lilia,* and went back to washing.

Jax scowled at him. "You like everybody."

True, but I like Lilia a lot, he said cheerfully.

Jax sat down heavily on her bed. "I like her too," she sighed. "The problem is she thinks best friends should tell each other everything. But I can't exactly tell her everything, can I? 'Ooh, Lilia, sorry I can't come round tonight, I've got to go home and help my magic moon cat with his secret mission.' It's like I'm living a double life, Beans!"

Jax was interrupted by a sudden unbelievable din coming from downstairs.

 Someone was pressing the café's doorbell and hammering on the door at the same time. It was seven in the morning, too early for customers.

Mum hurried down. "Okay, okay, I'm coming!"

Jax rushed after her to see what was going on. She was startled to see Ruby-Rose's mum on the step. She didn't look like she'd escaped from a catalogue this morning. She hadn't even combed her hair.

"Could you put up one of these? My daughter's little dog has gone missing." She held up a poster with a photograph of a worried-looking Betty Boo. At the top it said: *HAS ANYBODY SEEN THIS DOG?*

"Of course," said Mum. "How long has she been missing?"

"Since last night. My husband thinks she ran out while he was getting something out of the car."

"Has she run away before?" asked Mum.

"Never." Ruby-Rose's mum sounded scornful. "She hasn't got enough intelligence. She got out by mistake and now she's too dim to find her way back home."

Jax scowled at her from behind Mum's back. Some people shouldn't be allowed to have dogs.

"It was my husband's idea to have a dog," Ruby-Rose's mum said, as if she'd read Jax's mind. "I think he's regretting it now, though, with the amount of money she's costing us at the vet's. The vet told us her fur keeps coming out because she's stressed. I said, 'She's a dog! What's she got to be stressed about?' I'm the one that's chasing about after her, plus I've got to get Ruby-Rose ready for her big audition."

"You have got a lot on your plate," Jax's mum said politely.

"Oh, they're bound to pick Ruby-Rose," her mum said at once. "The same agency used her voice in a big commercial last year. For Sparkle Fluff? You must have seen it. It was huge." She pushed some posters at Mum. "Ruby-Rose said we have to put them up everywhere. I don't suppose it will do any good." And with that, Ruby-Rose's mum went hurrying off down the road to the Red Hot Wok.

Mum was studying the photo on the poster. "I can't believe they called that poor animal Betty Boo. No wonder she looks so worried!"

Jax rushed upstairs to tell Beans about Betty Boo's sudden disappearance. But when she ran into her room, it was empty. He must have slipped out on private business of his own.

Ruby-Rose didn't show up at school until morning break. Her face was red and puffy from crying.

Jax and Lilia discussed in whispers if they should try to comfort her. Lilia wasn't so keen. Ruby-Rose had recently thrown a full carton of juice at Lilia for no reason at all. "She's mean on a good day," she pointed out. "Who knows what she'll do now she's upset?"

"I don't like her either," Jax admitted. "But she really loves her dog. Just think if it was your Poppy and Petal that went missing."

Lilia didn't have to think about it. She and her mum were crazy about their cats. "We'll go over to her right now," she said at once.

"If she has a hissy fit just ignore her," said Jax.

"Unless she throws stuff," said Lilia.

But they never got the chance to comfort Ruby-Rose. As they watched, she fished her mobile out of her pocket and started pacing the playground as she talked. They heard her say, "Did you put posters on all the telegraph poles? Did you phone the Rescue Home like Dad said? Mum, why not? Someone could have handed her in! *Call* them, okay!"

On the way home, Lilia said, "Well, that was like a world record for Ruby-Rose. She didn't say one spiteful thing to anyone all day!"

"She didn't speak to anyone all day, that's why," Jax pointed out.

A car sped past them, screeching to a halt outside Suzie Dazzle's School for the Performing Arts. Inside were Ruby-Rose and her mum.

Ruby-Rose's mum leaned over her daughter to open the passenger door. Ruby-Rose seemed reluctant to get out, but at last she went trudging up the steps of the church with her dance bag.

Her mum called out of the car window.

"Remember what Suzie said! 'Eyes and teeth!' You've got a great smile, sweetie – use it!"

Jax couldn't believe it. If that was Jax she'd have been screaming, "I just lost my dog. DON'T tell me to smile, okay!" But Ruby-Rose just said wearily, "Okay, Mum."

Jax and Lilia watched Ruby-Rose's mum in disapproving silence as she drove away. "If Poppy and Petal went missing, I wouldn't be able to smile," Lilia said in a shocked voice. "Nor would my mum."

When they walked into the café, Mum was looking baffled.

"Any idea who or what smashed up our cat flap?" she demanded.

"Hello, Jax, hello, Lilia, have you had a nice day?" said Jax.

"Hello, Ellie Mae, hello, Lilia. Any idea who, or what, smashed up our brand-new cat flap

68

that I just had fitted at great expense?" Mum reeled off, but she and Jax were both laughing now.

"Hey, don't look at us! We've been stuck in school all day. Anyway, me and Lilia wouldn't fit through," Jax teased her. She couldn't help smirking to herself. It looked as if Beans had finally got his revenge on the evil cat-flap monster.

Lilia's mum had made cakes for Jax and Lilia that looked like little chocolate-covered mobile phones. They clowned around, pretending to phone each other, then they went upstairs to look for Moonbeans.

Jax was the first through her bedroom door, so she was the first to see an astonishing sight.

Moonbeans was curled up on her bed, purring his tea-kettle purr and looking unusually pleased with himself. Curled up beside him was a trembling but defiant Betty Boo.

I just don't get Ruby-Rose

5

Jax did some fast thinking. "Wow, look, Lilia!" she cried. "Clever little Beans has found Betty Boo – isn't that amazing?"

While Lilia rushed to coo over the little dog, Jax had a speedy talk with Beans. "What were you *thinking*, bringing her in through the cat flap?" she hissed. "How did she even fit through?"

It wasn't that hard. Betty Boo is mostly fluff. Beans seemed hurt. *I thought you'd be pleased to see her safe and sound.*

Jax was instantly ashamed. "No, I am. Sorry, Beans. Where did you find her?"

Beans had found Betty Boo wandering down by the old box factory near the canal. She was hungry and frightened, but had totally refused to go back home until Jax and Moonbeans promised to help Ruby-Rose.

"I thought you promised her last night?" she whispered.

You'd just been saying you weren't very fond of Ruby-Rose. I told her I wasn't sure you'd want to help.

Jax opened her mouth, then quickly closed it, surprised to discover that she had changed her mind about Ruby-Rose. She wasn't any fonder of Ruby-Rose, but she liked her dog, and Ruby-Rose was Betty Boo's human. *Betty Boo can't be happy until Ruby-Rose is happy,* Jax realized. *If that poor little dog gets any more stressed, she'll go totally bald! The Aunts were right, they both need our help.*

She leaned closer to Beans. "Of course I'll help," she whispered. "Tell Betty Boo it's sorted."

But it seemed that Betty Boo already knew. The words were hardly out of Jax's mouth before the little dog flipped onto her back, all four paws sticking up in the air, and let her tongue loll out in a foolish doggie grin.

"Oh, how *cute!*" said Lilia, laughing.

Jax felt her eyes prickle with tears. Ruby-Rose was not a nice person. But this little dog loved her so much that she had spent the night wandering the streets so she could get her human the magical help she needed.

73

"You're a good, brave little dog," she whispered. "Ruby-Rose is really lucky to have you."

In a louder voice she said, "I'd better tell Mum that Betty Boo is here. It's amazing my mum hasn't started sneezing. She's allergic to cats and dogs."

"Isn't she allergic to Moonbeans then?" asked Lilia.

"Actually, she isn't!" Jax flashed Lilia her most dazzling smile. "Isn't that weird?"

She sped downstairs to tell her mum that Ruby-Rose's dog was safe upstairs in her room. "She must have got lost and followed Moonbeans in through his cat flap." Jax quickly crossed her fingers as she told this white lie.

"Well, that clears up one mystery!" Mum said, laughing. She immediately phoned Ruby-Rose's family to tell them the news. There was no answer, so she left a message.

At 6.30 p.m. Mum pulled down the shutters and then she, Jax, Lilia and Lilia's mum ate supper together downstairs in the empty café. The mums swapped ideas for ways to improve the café; Lilia's mum, Nadia, suggested making a new line of cupcakes that would especially appeal to kids. "Good idea!" said Jax's mum, beaming. "Maybe we could hold a cupcake tasting evening for people from Goose Green School?"

Jax mostly tuned them out, chatting quietly with Lilia about stuff they liked to do. Jax said she wanted to take up karate again as soon as she found a good teacher. Lilia's passion was ice skating.

"I've never skated in my life," said Jax.

"You could come with us some time," Lilia said shyly.

It was only after Lilia and her mum had left that Jax realized no one had been to collect Betty Boo.

"I'll phone them again," Mum said through her yawns. It had been a busy day. "Maybe they didn't get my message." She was already calling the number. "There's cold chicken in the fridge," she told Jax. "If that little dog was out all night she must be starving."

Jax carried the plate of chicken scraps into her room. She tried not to look as Betty Boo hungrily golloped them down. Dogs could be seriously disgusting, she decided.

"I just don't get Ruby-Rose," she sighed to

Beans. "At school she's always stirring things up and causing trouble, but when she's with her mum she hardly opens her mouth. It's like she's two totally different girls."

Betty Boo said that since Ruby-Rose was picked to sing that Sparkle song, all her mum ever talks about is how they can make Ruby-Rose into a big star, Beans told her. *Ruby-Rose told Betty Boo that she doesn't feel like a person any more, she feels like a performing poodle.*

"Look, okay, so Ruby-Rose doesn't want to be a child star. Well, boohoohoo! Then she should just tell her parents!" Jax knew she wasn't being very sympathetic, but she couldn't really see a problem.

Beans looked at Betty Boo, who gave a sad little whimper. *Ruby-Rose says it's like her mum's big dream,* he translated.

Betty Boo suddenly jumped off the bed and

took off down the stairs like a rocket. Jax could hear her claws skittering on the bare wood as she went. A second later the doorbell buzzed. By the time Jax reached the hall, Betty Boo was flinging herself happily at a tired-looking man in blue overalls. *How did she know?* Jax thought, amazed.

"I just got home and found your message," Ruby-Rose's dad was telling Mum. "Down, Betty! Bad dog!" he scolded the madly leaping dog, but he was smiling. Ruby-Rose's dad and Betty Boo were both obviously happy to see each other, Jax thought.

Ruby-Rose should talk to her dad, Jax decided. *I bet he doesn't give a hoot if she's famous or not.*

That night, she couldn't sleep. After she had thumped her pillows a few times, Moonbeans said, *Are you worried about Ruby-Rose?*

"Yeah, I'm worried!" said Jax tetchily. "I'm worried because this is our first big mission for the Aunts and I haven't got a clue how we're going to help her."

She's a human like you. Talk to her, said Beans. *Get to know her.*

"How? At school, she looks right through me."

We just found her dog, said Moonbeans. *Ruby-Rose will be so grateful, she'll be your friend for ever.*

And pigs might fly, Jax thought. Moonbeans knew a lot about magic, but he knew absolutely nothing about Ruby-Rose!

Everybody needs
at least one friend

6

Jax was right. On Monday at school,
Ruby-Rose was stirring things up and having
huge hissy fits just like usual. She threw her
pencil case at Howard for absolutely no reason,
and told their teacher that Howard had started
it, because he was pulling mean faces.

"How could she even tell?" Jax whispered
to Lilia.

Howard's hair hung down over his face like
curtains. Some days you couldn't see his eyes,
or at least not both of them at the same time.
On Howard's one-eyed days, Jax longed to grab

a pair of scissors and help
him snip his way out.

But she and Beans were
on a mission for the Aunts, so at
break, Jax plucked up her courage and went up
to Ruby-Rose. "How is Betty Boo now after her
big scary adventure?" Jax was trying really hard
to be friendly.

"What's it got to do with you?" Ruby-Rose
snapped and she went stomping off.

"*Ooooh!*" giggled Lilia, who had been
watching. "That told you!"

"How am I going to help her if she won't
even talk to us?" Jax said in despair. Without
meaning to, she had spoken her thoughts
aloud.

"Why would you want to help Ruby-Rose?"
asked Lilia in surprise. "She didn't even say
thank you for finding her dog!"

Jax had to think fast. "This will sound really weird, but sometimes I get these sort of funny feelings, and I've got this really bad feeling about Ruby-Rose."

Lilia didn't think it was weird at all. "My granny's like you," she said cheerfully. "She always knows when something bad is going to happen. Do you think something bad is going to happen to Ruby-Rose?"

Jax shook her head. "I'm not sure."

They watched Ruby-Rose as she stormed across the playground, sending surprised little kids flying like skittles.

"You do realize she hasn't got a single friend," Jax said.

"Maybe she doesn't want friends," Lilia pointed out.

Jax had pretended she didn't need friends when she first came to Goose Green.

"Everybody needs at least one friend," she said.

"That's true," Lilia admitted. "I was really lonely before you came."

"Ruby-Rose was basically all right then, wasn't she?" Jax asked. She remembered seeing Ruby-Rose skipping with Lilia and some other girls on her first day at her new school.

"She wasn't *so* bad when I first came," Lilia agreed. Lilia had only started at Goose Green Primary a few months before Jax. "She was mostly okay, until she did that commercial."

"It's weird," said Jax. "Some kids would show off like mad if they got put on TV."

"It was only her voice," Lilia pointed out. "You couldn't see it was Ruby-Rose."

"I know, but it's like she doesn't want anyone to ever talk about it. When her mum was going on about it in the café, Ruby-Rose looked like she just wanted to disappear."

Jax didn't hear a word their teacher said for the rest of that day. She was racking her brains for a way they could help Ruby-Rose.

"I can't get to know her if she won't talk to me, can I?" she moaned to Beans when she got home.

They were in the back garden in the sunshine and Jax was tempting Beans with a piece of trailing string. She thought Beans was hilarious when he behaved like a normal kitten.

If she won't talk to you at school, Beans said, breathlessly chasing the string, *you'll just have to meet her outside school.*

Jax shook her head. "Ruby-Rose has this crazy schedule. Her mum is always rushing her off to auditions, tap-dancing and whatever."

84

Beans unexpectedly pounced, catching the string between his paws. *Then you'll have to take up tap-dancing,* he said calmly.

"Haha! Very funny!" Jax told him. "Can you seriously see me going tap, shuffle, hop? Anyway, she'll be in the top grade or something."

Doesn't Suzie Dazzle teach drama? asked Beans. *You told me you like drama.*

"Forget it!" she told him. "I'm not going to stupid Suzie Dazzle's! Have you seen the kids that go in there? All the girls are in pink!" Jax shuddered.

What's wrong with pink? Beans was refusing to let go of the string. He lay down with it trailing between his hind paws and gave it a sharp rabbit-kick to show it who was boss.

"It's what *kind* of pink," Jax said, still shuddering. "Suzie Dazzle's is the pukey kind."

*Then you'd better find something pukey pink to
wear or you won't blend in.* Beans was still grimly
hanging on to the string.

"I'm not going, so don't try to make me!" Jax
scrambled to her feet.

You promised Betty Boo we'd help her, said
Beans.

"I didn't say I'd totally humiliate myself,
though, did I?" Jax yelled over her shoulder as
she flounced inside.

Someone had posted a pile of fliers through
the side door. They scattered behind her like
fallen leaves as she raced up the stairs. Beans
only followed her as far as the downstairs hall.
She heard him start to purr.

The stairwell began to turn a deep
shimmering pink.

What's that moon kitten playing at? Jax
thought crossly. She glanced over the banisters

and was astonished to see the scattered fliers swirling towards her like a paper storm. She ducked, but the fliers had already whizzed harmlessly past – except for one, which fluttered enticingly around her head until she got mad and made a grab for it.

It was a voucher for a free lesson with Suzie Dazzle.

Jax is scarlet and gold

7

One week later, Jax came home from school and quickly changed into her "Suzie Dazzle" outfit; pukey pink leggings and a white T-shirt with pink writing that said *Cute as a Button*. Though the weather was still warm, she pulled lacey pink leg warmers on over her leggings. Jax had inherited these useful hand-me-downs from her cousins. She had refused to wear them until today.

Jax looked down at herself and shuddered. She still couldn't believe she was going through with this.

Feet! She thought in a sudden panic. *What do stage-school kids wear on their feet?* In the end, she put on her old suede ankle boots.

Finally she produced two pink hairbands that she'd had to borrow from Lilia. Screwing up her face, she dragged her hair into straggly bunches. Jax had totally the wrong hair for bunches. "I'm not wearing ribbons, okay?" she snapped at Beans. Jax had promised him she would try to fit in with the Suzie Dazzle kids, but she absolutely drew the line at ribbons.

"And if I hate it, we can come home, right?" she asked Beans for the umpteenth time.

Are you taking this seriously or not? he asked.

"Yes I am taking it seriously, thank you very much! Why do you think I'm dressed up like stage-school Barbie! Stop nagging, you bossy moon cat, and turn yourself invisible – we've got five minutes."

She and Moonbeans had a deal. If Jax had to humiliate herself at Suzie Dazzle's, Beans would come along as her invisible sidekick and do his Purr of Power. That way, with a little bit of moon magic to help things along, Ruby-Rose might actually let Jax talk to her.

Beans closed his eyes and vanished in a heartbeat.

Jax was impressed. "That was *smooth*. You've been practising!" She glanced in the mirror and swallowed hard. *I promise we will never have to do this again*, she told her dismayed reflection.

"Ready, partner?" she said aloud.

Ready, said her invisible sidekick.

Jax went to find her mum to let her know she was going.

Mum was talking to someone on the phone, so Jax just mouthed, "I'm going now, Mum," and her mum gave her a little wave.

She looked upset, Jax thought. Jax heard her say, "Ellie Mae and I were so disappointed you couldn't make it. I know you're busy, Dad, but we'd really love to see you."

Poor Mum, thought Jax. But she didn't have time to worry about Mum or Grandpa now. In exactly three minutes, she was going undercover at Suzie Dazzle's School for the Performing Arts.

Jax was welcomed at the door by a smiling teenage helper who said her name was Mimi. Mimi wore a frayed black top, black leggings, and earrings like little grinning skulls.

Jax guessed you had to be at least fifteen to get away with skulls at Suzie Dazzle's.

She shyly handed in her voucher. Mum had filled it in for her.

"Ellie Mae," Mimi read out. "What a pretty name! Have you done any acting before, Ellie Mae?"

Jax shook her head. "That's why I wanted to have the free lesson, to see if I like it."

This was the story she and Beans had agreed on. She could feel him weaving invisibly around her ankles.

"Trust me, if you've got talent, Suzie will sniff it out," Mimi said cheerfully. "Do you know any of the other kids here?"

"I *kind of* know Ruby-Rose," Jax admitted. Suddenly spotting Ruby-Rose halfway down the large hall she gave a hopeful wave, but Ruby-Rose immediately turned her back, making Jax feel foolish. "It's not working, let's go," she hissed to Beans.

We just got here, he pointed out.

Suzie Dazzle's School for the Performing Arts had once been a church, and the sunlight streaming through the stained glass windows cast lovely jewel colours everywhere.

Jax could hear two girls talking about a photo shoot they'd done for a kids' catalogue. Both girls wore shiny name necklaces. One girl was called Pixie and her friend was called Honey.

Jax had got her look almost right, she thought with relief; well, apart from her boots. The other girls wore black jazz shoes which made them walk like little flat-footed ducks.

There were only two boys in the class. They just wore ordinary T-shirts and jeans, Jax noticed enviously.

Until now, Suzie Dazzle had been standing at the back of the hall, chatting quietly on her mobile. Now she came hurrying towards Mimi, tapping her watch; time to start.

Mimi must have said something about the new girl, because Suzie turned and gave Jax a smile that was every bit as dazzling as her name.

Suzie was older than Jax had imagined. She had a wonderful voice, warm and slightly husky, that carried right across the hall.

"Come here, chickens," she called. "I want to introduce you all to Ellie Mae." Everyone gathered round, looking curiously at Jax, who felt herself going bright red.

"We'll start with our clapping game so Ellie Mae can learn all your names," Suzie told them.

She made them stand in a ring and take it in turns to introduce themselves. You didn't just have to say your name, you had to clap out the beats at the same time. Then, before the next person introduced themselves, they had to clap out and say your name and the names of all the other people who came before you.

Jax came third so she only had to remember two other names, Lulu and Kitty. She felt really sorry for the person at the end, who had to remember a string of twenty or more names.

Next they did warm-up exercises, running around the room and yelling out silly noises like "Me, ma, mo, me." Suzie said this was to get their voices working properly.

Then Mimi put on some loud music. *Good,* thought Jax. Now Beans could do his Purr of Power without anyone hearing.

The next exercise was like one of those musical party games. As soon as the music stopped you had to shake hands with the nearest person and introduce yourself, except this time you had to say a number instead of your name. Suzie said they had to decide if they wanted their number to sound exciting, creepy, comical, or mushy and romantic.

Jax picked 999 for her number. She decided her number was extremely creepy. "I am 999," she announced spookily every time the music stopped. She put on a hollow voice as if she was speaking from inside a coffin.

One of the boys, Marcus, seemed to think that acting was the same as shouting. "I am FIIIVE!" he bellowed into her face.

Hadley, the other boy, had such a quiet voice that she had no clue what his number was.

Kitty had decided that her number was really upset. She ran around wringing her hands like a heroine on a sinking ship. "I am one!" she sobbed. "I am one and I am *all* alone!"

"Just tell us the number, chicken!" Suzie told her briskly. "You know the rules by now."

Jax never found out what number Ruby-Rose had chosen, because Ruby-Rose was careful to keep on the opposite side of the hall, as far away from Jax as possible.

Suzie and Mimi were watching all the children carefully during these exercises. Occasionally they called someone out, and got them to try a different tone of voice or a different expression. But Suzie never called

Jax out. When she heard Jax do her spooky coffin voice, she said, "That's *fabulous*, darling! Well done!"

Pixie shot Jax a spiteful look. "Suzie's only praising her because she's new," she hissed to Honey. "She doesn't actually think she's any good."

"Why don't you fly off back to Fairyland, little Pixie?" Jax said under her breath.

Then Suzie made them play a different version of the same game. This time instead of numbers, they had to be colours.

"I am scarlet and gold," Jax called out every time the music stopped.

"I am baby b-b-blue," Kitty choked, still wringing her hands.

"I am deepest darkest midnight BLACK!" Marcus shouted into Jax's face. Only one of those words was a colour, but she didn't point this out.

At the end of the colours game, Jax realized that she had shaken hands with everyone else in the drama group except Ruby-Rose. It was almost like Ruby-Rose was deliberately avoiding her, she thought.

Suzie told them to take a ten-minute break. Jax suddenly felt Moonbeans rubbing up against her ankle boots. *Ruby-Rose only mixes with the other kids when Suzie tells her to,* he reported, *did you notice?*

Jax was frowning across the hall at Ruby-Rose. "Have you been doing the Purr of Power?"

Every time Suzie puts on the music. It's not working, is it?

99

By scrunching up her eyes super-tight, Jax could just make out a very feeble glow surrounding Ruby-Rose like a fuzzy halo. Usually, when Beans did the Purr of Power everything went shimmery fiery pink. But he was right, Jax thought, bewildered. This time his magic wasn't working. Something must be interfering with the moon vibes because they were having no effect on Ruby-Rose whatsoever.

"This hall is actually quite big," she comforted him.

It's not the hall, he said.

"What is it then?"

I don't know.

After the break, Suzie put on different kinds of music. They had to listen carefully, then move around in the style of the music.

What are we, four? thought Jax, as they

tiptoed about to tinkly fairy music, then stomped like elephants to clumpy piano sounds.

Jax decided she'd have to give herself a nosebleed so she and Beans could go home. Usually she just had to think about having one really hard and it came. She was about to get started when Suzie switched the rules. Now they had to be mighty warriors storming along to tinkling fairy music. They'd just got the hang of that when she yelled at them to switch again. Now they had to be romantic heroes and heroines wafting around to clumpy elephant music. Everybody ended up in fits of laughter; everyone except Ruby-Rose.

At last Suzie asked them to pair up with someone.

It was now or never and Jax didn't hesitate. As if the Aunts had prodded her in the back, she marched across the hall and grabbed a startled Ruby-Rose.

"Now one of you is going to be A and the other one is B," Suzie told them in her husky voice. "Sort that out between you now."

"I'll be A if that's okay," said Jax.

Ruby-Rose just shrugged. "Fine."

"Now I want all the As to pick someone in your life who is difficult to get on with."

I'm standing right next to her, thought Jax.

"Now all the Bs are going to play the part of that difficult person and I want the two of you to try to have a conversation."

Jax couldn't exactly tell Ruby-Rose to be Ruby-Rose, so she picked the next most difficult person in her life.

"You're my grandpa," she told Ruby-Rose.

"What's he like?" she asked in a bored voice.

Jax suddenly didn't feel like talking about her family to Ruby-Rose, but Suzie Dazzle was listening, so she mumbled, "He never comes to see us and it makes my mum really upset."

"Now you be Grandpa," Suzie told Ruby-Rose.

Ruby-Rose immediately turned herself into a bent old man out of a cartoon. She even had an imaginary stick.

"He isn't that old," said Jax, "and he doesn't have a stick. He is really grumpy, though."

Suzie told Jax to ask her grandpa why he was so grumpy.

"Why are you so grumpy, Grandpa?" Jax could feel her cheeks getting hot. This was embarrassing.

"What are you talking about, Ellie Mae? I'm not grumpy!" Ruby-Rose said in such a grumpy voice that Jax actually let out a giggle.

"That's just what he'd say," she told Suzie.

"Now you say something back," Suzie said. "Something friendly."

"Um, it was good you came to Mum's launch," she told Ruby-Rose shyly. "It meant a lot to her."

Ruby-Rose just glanced grumpily at her watch.

Jax didn't know what to say now, so she said awkwardly, "Actually, me and Mum would really love to see you more often."

"Yeah, well I have got a life of my own, you know," grumbled Ruby-Rose as Grandpa, and she sneaked another look at her watch. "Is it that time already? I can't stand about chatting. I've got something really important to do."

Though Jax knew they were both

pretending, she suddenly lost her temper. "Well, fine!" she shouted. "Do your really important thing. Me and Mum don't need you, so there!" And she stormed off. She was almost crying when she felt Suzie gently touch her arm.

"Now turn around," she whispered.

Very slowly, Jax turned round.

Ruby-Rose hadn't moved. She was staring after Jax. At that moment, she didn't look like a little girl; she looked like a sad old man. "Don't go," she whispered. "Please don't go, Ellie Mae."

For a moment there was dead silence. Then Ruby-Rose ran off to the far side of the hall and wouldn't look at Jax for the rest of the lesson.

"She's a good actor," Jax told Beans as they walked home.

But you didn't make friends?

She shook her head. "Nope."

Jax had worn pukey pink leggings in public and tiptoed around to fairy music. Beans had purred until he was hoarse – and it had all been a total waste of time! Their efforts had made no impression on Ruby-Rose whatsoever.

"How was Suzie Dazzle's?" Mum asked when Jax got home.

"It was okay. Mum, can I phone Lilia? I need to ask her something."

When Lilia picked up the phone, Jax could hear loud music and clattering cooking sounds in the background. "Hi, how did it go at Suzie D's?" Lilia asked her cheerfully.

"Not too well," Jax confessed.

"Have you still got a bad feeling about Ruby-Rose?"

"Worse," said Jax. "That's why I'm phoning you."

"Me?" said Lilia. "What can I do?"

"We need to help Ruby-Rose find some friends, and you always have really cool ideas," Jax said, realizing that this was true.

"Do I?" Lilia gave an amazed giggle. "Guess I'd better come up with a REALLY cool idea now! Hang on. I'm going to have a think."

Lilia went quiet for a few minutes, then she said, "Remember when I was at yours last week? My mum asked your mum if they should maybe try out a new line of cupcakes aimed just at kids. Your mum said they could have a tasting evening for people from our school. Maybe you could get your mum to invite Ruby-Rose for, like, a *practice* tasting session? Invite me too, and Conrad, because he's a laugh, and you should probably invite some other kids so it doesn't look too suspicious."

Jax felt a smile starting up somewhere inside. She was right. Lilia had really cool ideas. "Would she come, though?" she asked anxiously.

"Jax, I keep telling you. Your café is the coolest place in Goose Green! Why wouldn't she come?"

Jax felt herself blushing. "Honestly?"

"Ask anyone," said Lilia.

"Lilia's had a totally genius idea!" Jax told Moonbeans when they were alone in her room, and she told him what Lilia had suggested.

She had just started to peel off her Suzie Dazzle clothes when she had an alarming thought. "Beans! The cupcakes will be gone in, like, fifteen minutes! What will we do then?"

Beans smoothly turned his head until he was facing one of the three photos Jax kept beside her bed – the one of her in her fighter-girl clothes.

You could teach them karate, he said.

The cupcake and karate party

8

When Jax suggested inviting a few kids from her school to try out Nadia's new cupcakes, her mum was thrilled. But before they invited anyone else, Jax got her mum to phone up Ruby-Rose's mum to ask if Ruby-Rose could take time out from her busy schedule to take part in the tasting.

"She'd be doing us a huge favour," Mum told her. "We don't want to make cakes for children that they don't actually like!"

Jax waited on tenterhooks for her mum to get off the phone.

"Is she coming?"

"She says Ruby-Rose can spare us an hour. Imagine being that busy when you're nine!" Mum sighed. "Oh, and she said, would I please make sure her daughter didn't eat too many cakes!"

When Jax got home on the afternoon of the party, her mum and Nadia were already setting out the café tables with cakes and soft drinks. Before she and Lilia had moved to Goose Green, Nadia had worked in a swanky bakery, and she was always coming up with funky new designs for cakes and cookies. This time she'd baked some robot cupcakes, some of the mobile-phone cakes she'd made for Lilia and Jax, Lego

 sponge cakes that Nadia
had iced with red, blue
and yellow icing so they
looked as if they were
built from real
Lego bricks, cakes decorated
to look like little pizzas, and
some cupcakes topped with
cute marshmallow dogs that
looked exactly like Betty Boo.

Jax had just decided that the Betty Boo cakes
were her new favourites, when Nadia smilingly
set down a plate containing just one giant iced
 cupcake, topped with a skinny
marzipan kitten with huge
yellow-gold eyes.

"It's Moonbeans!" Jax
gasped. "You made a
Moonbeans cake!"

"Three kinds of chocolate; your favourite," Nadia said, ruffling her hair. "I made that one for you. Lilia told me the two of you are trying to make friends with Ruby-Rose. You are a kind girl, Ellie Mae."

Jax felt her cheeks getting hot as she remembered Lilia almost crying in the street. She wasn't always kind to Lilia, and she'd never have tried to make friends with Ruby-Rose if the Aunts hadn't made her. But she couldn't say this to Lilia's mum, so she just said, "You've made Moonbeans look exactly right."

"Your mum always says he looks like a little space alien," Nadia said, laughing. "Those great big eyes!"

"Ha ha ha!" Jax laughed back nervously.

The door opened and Ruby-Rose walked into the café. Jax had told everyone to come in old comfy clothes. Of course, Ruby-Rose's

mum wouldn't dream of letting her daughter go out in old clothes, so Ruby-Rose was wearing a peach satin party dress with matching satin shoes.

Jax had invited two other girls from school, called Jasmine and Bella. Their faces lit up when they saw the cakes. "Are we allowed to eat as many as we like?" Jasmine breathed.

"Sure," said Jax, laughing. "You just have to tell us which are your favourites."

Conrad arrived last, wearing jogging trousers and an old T-shirt.

When he spotted the cakes his eyes almost popped out of his head. "You're lucky I could come!" he said cheekily. "I can see you girls are going to need a LOT of help!"

"Oh, yeah!" Lilia said, sticking out her tongue. "I bet we can eat more cupcakes than you!"

"Want to bet?" Conrad demanded.

Jasmine, Bella and Lilia immediately accepted Conrad's cupcake challenge and started cramming cakes into their mouths. Ruby-Rose was standing all by herself. She had hovered frowningly over all the plates of cupcakes for ages before eventually picking out a mobile-phone cake. But the next time Jax looked she'd put it down uneaten.

"Do you want to help me keep score?" Jax asked her.

Ruby-Rose silently shook her head.

For the next ten minutes, the only sound was munching and swallowing, interrupted by friendly insults between Conrad and the girls.

Afterwards, Lilia and Jax agreed that it probably wasn't clever to let Conrad have so much sugar. After he'd scoffed down two robot cakes, a Lego cake and a cupcake that looked exactly like a tiny pepperoni pizza, Conrad started clowning about in the way that drove their teacher mad.

Jax glanced anxiously at Ruby-Rose. She had gone to stand by the door to the café, looking bored, as if she was waiting for her mum.

"Quick, do the Purr of Power!" she hissed to Beans. "Ruby-Rose wants to leave; it's all going wrong!"

I'm trying, he told her.

Jax squinted around the café. Beans's magic was working better than at Suzie Dazzle's –

the air had gone ever so slightly
shimmery – but that was all.

"Did you tell the Aunts
that your magic keeps going
wrong?" she asked Beans.

Yes, it's not my magic, it's Ruby-Rose.

"What do you mean?"

*Ruby-Rose needs to do something before my
magic can work,* Beans explained.

"Something like what?"

*The Aunts said it's something only Ruby-Rose
knows.*

"So your moon magic isn't working on her
at all?"

Does it look like it's working? Beans asked.

Nothing worked with Ruby-Rose, Jax
thought; Nadia's fabulous cupcakes didn't work,
finding Betty Boo didn't work, being friendly
didn't work. It was like Ruby-Rose was

surrounded by some kind of prickly force field. Everything bounced off her; even magic. It would be another three quarters of an hour before Ruby-Rose's mum came to collect her. Jax couldn't let her stand there by herself staring out of the window. She had to do something.

She felt Moonbeans brush against her ankles. He was purring.

This isn't just a cupcake party, remember, he told her.

"Oh yeah," she breathed. "Thanks, Beans!" In her panic, Jax had forgotten all about the karate.

She jumped up from the table and clapped her hands. "Okay, I'm taking you all next door to teach you some karate!" she announced. Her voice was slightly squeaky with nerves, but nobody seemed to notice.

Conrad broke into a huge grin. "Wicked!"

Ruby-Rose was so surprised she actually giggled. "*Cool!* A karate party!" Her face suddenly fell. "I don't think I can do karate in this dress."

But Jax wasn't going to let a silly dress get in the way of a good plan. "I've got an old karate outfit you can borrow," she told her.

There was a room behind the café which Mum had said they could use. She'd made Jax promise not to teach them anything dangerous, so she just took them through some basic warm-up exercises. Then, when she thought they were ready, she taught them the simple trick that had totally blown her away when she started learning karate.

"Mmm, who shall I pick to help me?" she said thoughtfully. "I think I'll pick Ruby-Rose. Will you come out to the front, please?"

She told Ruby-Rose to hold her arm out really stiffly, then the others had to try to push it down. Bella, Jasmine, Lilia and Conrad were all able to push her arm down straight away. "That was easy!" Conrad complained. "Next task, please, and make it much harder!" He started jogging on the spot, flexing his muscles.

"We haven't finished!" said Jax in her sternest voice and Conrad instantly stopped jogging.

Next Ruby-Rose had to hold her arm more loosely, and again all the others were able to push it down straight away.

Ruby-Rose started to look hot and bothered. "How come they all did that so easily? I must be doing something wrong."

"Hey, relax, girl," Jax told her, grinning. "I haven't showed you the really cool part yet!" She asked Ruby-Rose to hold her arm just normally, not too tense or too relaxed, and then to imagine that she had turned on a tap and pure cosmic energy was pouring through her arm and out into the universe.

In the sudden hush, Jax heard Moonbeans purring somewhere nearby. "Try to push her arm down now," she told Conrad.

He pushed and pushed till he was red in the face. "It won't budge!" he said, amazed. "Ruby-Rose has suddenly got really strong!"

Lilia tried next. She couldn't push Ruby-Rose's arm down either.

Ruby-Rose's eyes had gone huge. "I *felt* it, Jax! Cosmic energy came whooshing down my arm, just like you said!"

"Is it magic?" Lilia asked in awe.

Jax laughed. "No, silly, it's karate!"

"Karate does sometimes look a lot like magic, though," said Conrad, and Jax knew he was remembering the time she turned into a flashing, sparkling girl firework.

At the end of the karate party all the children were flushed and breathless, but Ruby-Rose's face absolutely glowed.

"She's smiling!" Jax whispered to Lilia. "She's even *laughing*!"

"I *know*!" Lilia whispered. "I almost like her! Do you think she'd come skating?"

"Ask her," said Jax.

Ruby-Rose's eyes lit up when Lilia invited her to come skating with them. Then the sparkle faded from her eyes. "Mum says my diary is really full. There's the audition for the commercial, then I'm auditioning for a part in the Goose Green Christmas panto."

Jax had just spent thirty minutes telling other children what to do. Without thinking, she said bossily, "Ruby-Rose, you know you hate all this child star stuff. Just tell your mum you're not doing it."

For a moment Ruby-Rose actually wrung her hands, like Kitty at Suzie Dazzle's. "I can't tell my mum." Her eyes were bright with tears.

"Then tell your dad. Your dad's really sensible."

"He's never home," Ruby-Rose said despairingly. "He's just started up his own garage. He has to work really hard."

Lilia put an arm around her shoulders. "You've got to talk to them, Ruby."

"Sweetie! What's happened to your beautiful party dress?"

Ruby-Rose's mum had arrived ten minutes early to collect Ruby-Rose. She looked at her barefoot daughter in horror. "And you're all flushed!" She quickly felt Ruby-Rose's forehead. "I hope you're not going down with something, not with these auditions coming up. Not to mention your birthday is only two weeks away. You've still got to decide what you want for your party!"

Ruby-Rose silently changed back into her party clothes. "Thanks for having me, Mrs. Jackson," she said to Jax's mum, and she sounded like a girl robot. "The cupcakes were extremely delicious."

"Thanks for having me," echoed Conrad. "You know where I live next time you need a tester!"

Still in her karate clothes, Jax went out to say goodbye to her guests. Moonbeans came pattering out with her.

"I thought it was working," Jax said.

So did I, said Beans.

"Now I feel really depressed. Do you?"

Moonbeans didn't answer.

Jax watched Ruby-Rose and her mum hurrying down the street. At least, Ruby-Rose's mum was hurrying...Ruby-Rose seemed to be hanging back. Suddenly she turned. Jax thought she was going to wave, but she was gazing back at the Dream Café with such a bleak expression that Jax wanted to run after her and shake her and shout, "Forget about your mum and her big dream! What about *your* dream? When are you going to fight back, Sparkle Fluff Girl?"

Jax gasped. She had just understood why

125

Moonbeans's magic wouldn't work on Ruby-Rose. "Beans, I know what she needs to do!" she told him excitedly. "I finally figured out how to help Ruby-Rose!"

Next day at morning break, Lilia and Jax went up to Ruby-Rose.

When the whistle went twenty minutes later, the three girls were still in a tight huddle, all talking at once. Together they had come up with a plan.

That evening, for the first time ever, Ruby-Rose phoned Jax. She sounded nervous but excited. "I did it! I did it just how you said. I told my mum I want to have my birthday party at the Dream Café. I said we'd be the first people to book your café for a party. I think she liked that."

"Did you tell her about…you know?" asked Jax.

Ruby-Rose let out a mischievous giggle. "Did I tell my mum about me teaching you all a dance sequence in our lunch hour to perform for everyone in the café? Duh! Of course I told her."

It was true that Lilia, Jax and Ruby-Rose were practising something in their lunch hour, but it wasn't a dance sequence, and it wasn't Ruby-Rose doing the teaching. It was Jax. She was teaching Lilia and Ruby-Rose a series of simple karate moves called a *kata*.

When they got their moves right, their *kata* did look like a graceful dance; a ferocious, swooping, gliding, kicking war-dance.

After the first session, Lilia and Ruby-Rose started jumping about, aiming pretend punches at each other.

"Stop that, both of you!" Jax said at once.

Lilia looked surprised. "We were just messing around, Jax."

"I should have said this before," Jax said apologetically. "My karate teacher made us promise that we would never ever use karate to hurt anybody. I need you to make the same promise."

"I promise," said Ruby-Rose at once.

"So do I," said Lilia humbly. "Sorry, Jax."

The second time they met up in their special corner of the playing field, Conrad was waiting with a stony expression. "How come you didn't ask me to join your little private group?" he demanded.

"Sorry, girls only," Ruby-Rose told him.

Conrad looked genuinely hurt. "How come? I should be here more than you. I've wanted to learn karate for ever, haven't I, Jax?"

Jax nodded. Conrad had been on at her
to teach him ever since that day in the
playground, when she'd turned into a
karate-kicking girl firework.

"Let him stay," sighed Lilia. "It'll look better
if there's more of us."

"If he promises not to mess it up," said
Ruby-Rose.

"He'll promise, won't you, Conrad?" Lilia
patted his shoulder and he grinned and
nodded.

"These are my rules," Jax told Conrad in her
fiercest voice. "Absolutely NO clowning about!
You do not make up your own karate moves
and you don't yell out 'HA!' just because you
feel like it! Do you swear?"

Conrad nodded solemnly. "I swear."
Then he grinned at Jax. "I've thought up a

great name for our group: The Goose Green
Karate Kickers!"

At home, Jax noticed Mum was getting
nervous. Not counting the launch, Ruby-Rose's
party was the first real party they'd held in their
café.

Ruby-Rose had only invited a few kids from
school, plus her little cousins, aunties
and uncles, and her mum and
dad, but being Ruby-Rose
she wanted pretend
cocktails decorated with

fruit and
parasols, and
about a billion kinds
of party nibbles.

Lilia's mum was going to
bake a special birthday cake.

131

 Jax had told Ruby-Rose to order the one with three different types of chocolate. "Have you heard of that pudding called Death by Chocolate?" she'd asked her. "Nadia's chocolate cake is like that, only with *way* more chocolate!"

The party was going to be after school. The Goose Green Karate Kickers were having their final rehearsal in the café's back room before the party started.

Jax and Beans had agreed that he'd be in the café to meet and greet Ruby-Rose's guests, getting a happy party vibe going with his moon magic before the Kickers came out.

After the rehearsal, all the Kickers quickly put on their costumes. The girls were wearing party frocks that Ruby-Rose had worn to various competitions. Jax thought Ruby-Rose's mum was going to have a fit when she saw how they had slit the dresses down the back and tacked on bits of velcro.

"Do our dresses look weird with our karate things underneath?" asked Ruby-Rose anxiously.

"Doesn't matter," said Jax. "They'll just be trying to figure out exactly what we're supposed to be, when—"

"BAM!" Conrad said, grinning. "We sock it to 'em!"

Conrad was looking unusually smart for Conrad, in black jogging trousers, a white shirt and a clip-on bow tie.

Jax's mum put her head around the door. "They're all here! Are you ready?"

Ruby-Rose suddenly grabbed Jax's hand. "I can't do it."

"Hey, Sparkle Fluff, don't be such a girl – get a grip!" Conrad told her. And to everyone's relief and surprise, Ruby-Rose got a grip.

The four children filed out into the centre of the café, where tables had already been cleared to make a space. Jax felt a big smile spread over her face. Beans must have been working overtime. The café was pink and sparkling with party vibes. All the guests wanted to make a fuss of the cute kitten with huge golden eyes.

At a nod from Jax, Lilia's mum turned on some pop music. This was Ruby-Rose's idea, so that her mum and the other guests would be fooled into thinking that Ruby-Rose and her school friends were going to do a normal dance routine. They bopped about to the pop music for maybe half a minute, then Jax gave Lilia's mum a nod and she switched on the real music. Jax had chosen Japanese music, because karate originally came from Japan. All the Kickers lined up and bowed solemnly to the guests, who were getting embarrassed and fidgety; what kind of a party was this?

"One, two, three," Jax said under her breath.

On "three", the girls all swung to point at Conrad, who ripped off his bow tie and his shirt and struck his fiercest karate pose. "Get ready to meet Goose Green's Karate Kickers!" he yelled.

With one quick flick, Lilia, Ruby-Rose and Jax unfastened the Velcro holding their shiny frocks together, revealing loose white karate outfits underneath.

Ruby-Rose's dad suddenly sat up straight. He looked surprised at first, then amused, then really proud, as his daughter and her new

 friends demonstrated the
kicks, punches, blocks
and throws that Jax had
made them practise in
their lunch hour. Their
performance ended
with all of them kicking
and stamping their way
towards the seated guests like fierce warriors.
Then at the last minute they stopped dead,
bowed extremely respectfully to the audience,
and the show was over.

When they finished, Ruby-Rose's dad, Jax's
mum and Lilia's mum clapped, cheered,
stamped and wolf-whistled. So did the aunts,
uncles, little cousins and the kids from school.

Ruby-Rose's mum sat silently with her hands
in her lap. She had looked surprised at first;
then she just looked angry.

Jax had hoped that doing karate in front of her mum would give Ruby-Rose courage, but Ruby-Rose wasn't actually looking that brave.

She looked more like she might be sick.

"Do the Purr," Jax hissed at Moonbeans.

Just wait, he told her.

Suddenly Ruby-Rose straightened her shoulders. "You didn't clap," she said, looking her mum in the eye. "Didn't you like it?"

"You said you were going to dance," her mum said in a tight voice. "You told me a fib."

Ruby-Rose took a shaky breath. "I told a fib because if I'd told you what we were really doing you'd have said it was a waste of time. If it doesn't make me famous, you won't let me do it."

"That's not fair!" her mum said angrily.

"No, you're not fair!" Ruby-Rose said, clenching her fists. "You loved me being the

Sparkle Fluff Girl so much, it's like you wanted me to stay being her for ever and ever!"

For a terrible moment, Jax thought Ruby-Rose's mum was going to storm out. Then she heard a familiar throbbing sound and went weak with relief. It was going to be okay. Moonbeans was purring, and this time the magic was working. Jax could feel it tingling in the roots of her hair. All around the café, you could see people start to relax again.

She did it, Jax thought. Ruby-Rose really did it! The magic was working because Ruby-Rose was finally fighting back.

Now, in front of everyone, Ruby-Rose respectfully told her parents what she wasn't going to do.

"I don't want to be famous. I don't want to be a singing mouse in the Christmas pantomime. I don't want to do commercials for cat food or Sparkle Fluff, or go to Suzie Dazzle's School for the Performing Arts four afternoons a week."

"What *do* you want to do?" asked her mum, bewildered.

Ruby-Rose held her arms out wide as if she wanted to hug the whole world. "I want to do *everything*! I want to take Betty Boo to the park. I want to make cupcakes with Lilia's mum. I want to go ice skating with Jax and Lilia, and play computer games." Ruby-Rose started to giggle. "And I want to karate kick Conrad in his backside," she added mischievously, "and make him fall over!"

"In your dreams, Sparkle Fluff," Conrad said cheerfully.

"There are so many things I want to do," Ruby-Rose told her mum. "I honestly haven't got time to be famous."

Ruby-Rose's dad cleared his throat. "She wants to be a kid," he told his wife gruffly. "Just a normal, ordinary kid."

Ruby-Rose suddenly threw her arms around her parents. "I'm sorry, Mum. Are you really disappointed?"

Her mum gave Ruby-Rose a tearful hug. "No, I'm sorry! I thought you wanted what I wanted. I suppose I just wanted you to have a wonderful life."

Then Jax's mum tactfully dimmed the lights and Lilia's mum carried in the cake she had made for Ruby-Rose's birthday.

When Jax saw it, she blinked in surprise. She'd seen the cake when Nadia brought it to the café earlier. It had looked beautiful – all Nadia's cakes

140

looked beautiful – but it hadn't looked like this.

"Moonbeans," she hissed. "What did you do to that cake?"

He blinked his amber-gold eyes. *I just added a pinch of moon magic.*

Jax thought it was more than a pinch.

It was a birthday cake out of a dream, shimmering and twinkling like a cake spun from moonlight and stardust.

In the middle, in sparkly writing, it said:

Happy 9th Birthday, Ruby-Rose. May All Your Dreams Come True.

 # A message from Annie

Dear Readers,

Like Ellie Mae Jackson I lived just with my mum. She didn't run a café that sold magical cupcakes, she went out to work as a secretary, and in the holidays I took care of myself most days. I was often lonely and longed for a pet.

One day, most unusually, my mum took a day off from her job and even more unusually she walked me to my village school. She said she had arranged to meet one of my teachers but didn't explain why. Unlike most country people in those days, this teacher owned a car. We waited patiently outside the school gates and eventually saw him driving very carefully along the road. He stopped in front of us and I was amazed to see a tiny but extremely confident tabby kitten riding in the passenger seat. I was even more amazed when my mum explained that this kitten was for me!

I called him Tinker and he was the next best thing to a magical moon cat. He adored me from the start and, when he grew older, often tried to follow me to school. He seemed to know what time I'd be coming home and was always waiting for me on the corner. I shared all my thoughts and worries with Tinker, just like Jax does with Moonbeans, and I was absolutely convinced that he understood everything I was telling him. Like Moonbeans, Tinker often had to go out roaming on private cat business. Then, during the night he would jump in through my bedroom window, smelling of earth and wild flowers, and curl up with me until morning. I have known dozens of wonderful cats and kittens since then but none of them have been quite as magical and special as Tinker...except Beans. I hope you'll love my magical moon cat as much as I do. As a special treat, we've added a sneak preview of the next book – ENJOY!

Love and moon dust,
Annie xxx

www.anniedaltonwriter.co.uk

Calling all Magical Moon Cat Fans!

Read on for a sneak preview of
Jax and Beans's next mission,

MOONBEANS AND THE
TALENT SHOW

But remember –
it's TOP SECRET!

There was a sudden rustling from the stage as
Mr. Tattersall, the headmaster, folded up his
sheet of paper. He had finished the week's
announcements. Breathing a sigh of relief, Jax
got ready for him to tell everyone to return to
their classrooms after assembly. Instead, he
beamed around at everyone. "I have one final
and very special announcement," he said.

She muffled a groan. Not *another*
announcement!

"You have all worked extremely hard this term," he told them, still beaming. "So your teachers and I decided that you deserve a reward. Goose Green Primary School is going to put on its first ever talent show!"

Everybody gasped. Well, almost everybody; Howard didn't gasp, but Jax felt him go super-still behind his hair, as if he was genuinely fascinated to know what Mr. Tattersall was going to say next. Jax thought this was surprising. Talent shows were about showing off in public – why would this super-shy boy be interested in showing off?

Can Jax and Beans help Howard discover his hidden talent?

Find out what happens next in

Moonbeans and the Talent Show

Deliciously delectable recipes from
THE DREAM CAFÉ

Sprinkle some moon-cat magic on your special day
with one of these perfect party cake recipes.

Moonbeans's Chocolate Party Cake

This chocolate cake can be cut up into lots
of squares, so it's perfect for feeding large groups of
friends – dig in!

FOR THE CAKE (serves 12-15)

You will need:

100g (4oz) self-raising flour

40g (1½oz) cocoa powder

1½ teaspoons of baking powder

150g (5oz) softened butter or soft margarine

150g (5oz) soft brown sugar

1 teaspoon of vanilla essence

3 tablespoons of milk

3 large eggs

FOR THE CHOCOLATE BUTTERCREAM

You will need:

100g (4oz) softened unsalted butter or margarine

175g (6oz) icing sugar

40g (1½oz) cocoa powder

1 tablespoon of milk

½ teaspoon of vanilla essence

You will also need a 27 x 18cm (11 x 7in) rectangular cake tin, and 75g (3oz) of white chocolate for drizzling.

1. Heat the oven to 180°C / Gas mark 4. Grease and line the tin. To do this, put the tin or tray on some baking parchment. Draw around it. Cut out the shape, cutting just inside the line. Wipe a little softened butter or cooking oil over the inside of the tin or tray, using a paper towel. Put the parchment shape in the bottom of the tin or tray.

2. Sift the flour, cocoa and baking powder in a big bowl. Put the butter and sugar in another bowl.

3. Beat the butter or margarine and sugar until pale and fluffy. Mix in the vanilla and milk.

4. Crack an egg into a cup. Tip it into the butter and sugar mixture. Add 1 tablespoon of the floury mixture. Beat well. Do this with each egg.

5. Add the rest of the floury mixture and stir it in gently, using a big metal spoon, moving it in the shape of a number 8.

6. Scrape the mixture into the tin and level the top with the back of a spoon. Bake for 30-35 minutes, until risen and springy.

7. When the cake is cooked, leave it in the tin for a few minutes, then turn it out onto a wire rack. To do this, run a knife around the tray to loosen the cake. Put a wire rack over the tray. Turn the tray and rack over

together, so the tray ends up on top. The cake should pop out onto the rack.

8. To make the buttercream, put the butter or margarine in a large mixing bowl and beat with a wooden spoon until it becomes soft and fluffy.

9. Mix the icing sugar and cocoa powder together. Sift in one third of the mix into the bowl and stir it in. Then, sift the rest of the icing sugar and cocoa powder over the mixture.

10. Add the milk and vanilla. Beat quickly, until you have a chocolatey, fluffy mixture.

11. When the cake is cold, spread the buttercream over the top.

12. Decorate the cake with drizzled chocolate. Melt the chocolate, and scoop it up with a spoon. Hold the spoon over the cake. Tip the spoon, then move it over the cake, leaving a trail of white chocolate.

Betty Boo Macaroons

contains nuts!

Ruby-Rose's mum is no stranger to luxury, and macaroons are the ultimate stylish party food. Made of whisked egg whites mixed with ground almonds, macaroons are baked so the outside goes crisp while the inside stays chewy. Yum!

FOR THE MACAROONS

(makes about 12 pairs of raspberry macaroons)

You will need:

100g (4oz) icing sugar

2 medium eggs

A pinch of cream of tartar

¼ teaspoon of pink food colouring

25g (1oz) caster sugar

100g (4oz) ground almonds

FOR BETTY BOO'S SPECIAL FILLING

You will need:

100g (4oz) fresh raspberries

150g (5oz) full-fat cream cheese

2 tablespoons of icing sugar

1. Line two large baking sheets with baking parchment. There are tips on how to do this in the first stage of the chocolate cake recipe. Sift the icing sugar into a bowl.

2. Separate the eggs. Put the egg whites in a large, clean bowl.

3. Whisk the egg whites until they stand up in peaks. Whisk in the cream of tartar, food colouring and 2 tablespoons of the icing sugar.

4. Add the rest of the icing sugar a tablespoon at a time, whisking well each time.

5. Add the caster sugar and ground almonds. Use a metal spoon to fold them in very gently. Remember to move the spoon in the shape of a number 8.

6. Scoop up almost a teaspoon of the mixture. Put it on the baking tray, using another spoon to push it off. Make more blobs, spacing them out well.

7. Tap each tray sharply on the work surface, twice. Leave for thirty minutes.

8. Heat the oven to 110°C / Gas mark ¼. Bake for 30 minutes. Then turn off the oven and leave the macaroons in for 15 minutes. Next, leave them on the trays to cool.

9. To make the filling, mash the raspberries with a fork. Stir in the cream cheese and icing sugar.

10. Spread some filling over the flat side of a macaroon. Press on another macaroon. Fill the rest in the same way. Yum!

FOR LEMON OR ORANGE MACAROONS

Use yellow food colouring for lemon macaroons, or half yellow and half red for orange macaroons. For the filling, replace the raspberries with the grated rind of 1 orange or lemon; mix in 2 tablespoons of juice squeezed from the fruit and a few drops of food colouring.

FOR MINT CHOCOLATE MACAROONS

Replace the pink food colouring with green, and add 4 drops of peppermint essence at the same time. Instead of the raspberry filling, make some chocolate ganache. Just melt 40g (1½oz) of plain or milk chocolate and stir in 2 tablespoons of double cream. Let this cool for 10 minutes, and put it in the fridge for 1 hour, stirring every now and then.

Goose Green Victoria Sponge Cake

There's nothing like a classic Victoria sponge cake to brighten any tea party. This magical moon-cat recipe uses pink buttercream for a unique Goose Green twist.

FOR THE SPONGE (makes 12 slices)

You will need:

225g (8oz) self-raising flour

225g (8oz) caster sugar

225g (8oz) soft margarine

4 medium eggs

FOR THE FILLING

You will need:

100g (4oz) softened butter or soft margarine

225g (8oz) icing sugar

1 tablespoon of milk

½ teaspoon of vanilla essence

A few drops of pink food colouring

4 tablespoons of strawberry jam

You will also need two 20cm (8in) round, shallow cake tins.

1. Heat the oven to 180°C /Gas Mark 4. Grease and line the tins. There are tips on how to do this in the first stage of the chocolate cake recipe.

2. Sift the flour into a big bowl. Add the sugar and margarine. Break an egg into a cup, then tip it into the bowl. Do the same with the other eggs.

3. Stir until you have a smooth mixture. Spoon half into each cake tin and smooth the tops with the back of the spoon.

4. Bake for 25 minutes, or until the cakes are risen and firm. Leave in the tins for 5 minutes.

5. Run a knife around the tins, then turn the cakes onto a wire rack.

6. Peel off the parchment. Turn the cakes the right way up. Then, make the buttercream.

7. For the buttercream, put the butter or margarine in a large mixing bowl and beat with a wooden spoon until it becomes soft and fluffy.

9. Sift one third of the icing sugar into the bowl and stir it in. Then, sift the rest of the icing sugar over the mixture.

10. Add the milk and vanilla essence, and just a couple of drops of pink food colouring to tint the buttercream. Beat quickly, until you have a pale-pink, fluffy mixture.

11. When the cakes are cool, put one on a plate, flat side up. Spread on the buttercream. Next spread 4 tablespoons of jam on top of the buttercream. Put the other cake on top, flat side down. Press gently. Sprinkle some caster sugar on top.

A delicious classic!

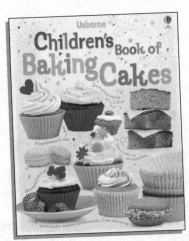

My Magical Moon Cat Page

Hello! It's me again, Jax! I hope reading about my latest mission has given you loads of ideas for your own special projects...

Jot down plans for your next TOP SECRET missions here.

_____

_____

_____

_____

_____

_____

_____

_____

_____

_____

_____

_____

_____

Add a touch of magic with your own space-tastic stickers!

_____